SCOOBY-DOO!

VERSUS THEM!

PAUL KUPPERBERG--WRITER FABIO LAGUNA--ARTIST
TRAVIS LANHAM--LETTERER DAVE TANGUAY--COLORIST
HARVEY RICHARDS--EDITOR VINCENT DEPORTER--COVER

Spotlight

visit us at www.abdopublishing.com

Reinforced library bound edition published in 2012 by Spotlight, a division of the ABDO Group, 8000 West 78th Street, Edina, Minnesota 55439. Spotlight produces high-quality reinforced library bound editions for schools and libraries. Published by agreement with Warner Bros.—A Time Warner Company. The stories, characters, and incidents mentioned are entirely fictional. All rights reserved. Used under authorization.

Printed in the United States of America, Melrose Park, Illinois.
052011
092011
This book contains at least 10% recycled materials.

Library of Congress Cataloging-in-Publication Data

Kupperberg, Paul.
  Scooby-Doo versus them! / writer, Paul Kupperberg ; artist, Fabio Laguna.
  -- Reinforced library bound ed.
      p. cm. -- (Scooby-Doo graphic novels)
  ISBN 978-1-59961-926-2
  1. Graphic novels. I. Laguna, Fabio, ill. II. Scooby-Doo (Television program) III. Title.
  PZ7.7.K87Sd 2011
  741.5'973--dc22

                        2011001376

All Spotlight books are reinforced library bindings
and manufactured in the United States of America.

SCOOBY-DOO!
Table of Contents

WE'VE FOUND *DOZENS* OF THESE WORM-HOLES COVERED IN THE *SAME* SLIME.

WE'VE ALSO GOTTEN REPORTS OF STRANGE NOISES FROM SOME OF THE *PROSPECTORS* THAT STILL WORK THE OLD MINES.

THANKS, TROOPER! WE'LL HAVE A LOOK AROUND AND SEE WHAT WE CAN COME UP WITH. LET'S GO, GANG!

GIANT WORMS... I WONDER HOW YOU'D *STOP* SOMETHING LIKE THAT?

MAYBE WITH, LIKE, A GIANT *FISH HOOK?*

HOLD ON THAR A SEC, PARDNERS!

SCREEEECH

CAN WE HELP YOU, SIR?

I SURE HOPE SO, BOY! MY NAME'S--

WOOLEY WEST-- OWNER OF WILD WOOLEY'S WESTLAND AMUSEMENT PARKS!

AT YER SERVICE! I'M ABOUT TO BUY UP THIS HERE GHOST TOWN TO TURN IT INTO MAH NEWEST AMUSEMENT PARK.

THEN I HEARD TELL SOME GIANT *WORM* ABOUT NEAR *WRECKED* THE PLACE.

DON'T WORRY, MR. WEST. WE'LL GET TO THE *BOTTOM* OF THIS!

WORRY?

TARNATION, GAL... I COULDN'T BE *HAPPIER!* THINK'A ALL THE *FREE PUBLICITY* THIS'LL GET ME!

'COURSE, THEM WORMS IS DOIN' ME A *FAVOR* BY *SCARIN'* EVERYONE-- --SO CAN'T *NO ONE* FIND WHAT *I* FOUND!

WHAT DID YOU FIND, MR. FENSTER?

THAT'S FOR *ME* T'KNOW AND FOR YOU... *NOT* TO FIND OUT! HEH HEH! ADIOS, AMIGOS!

LATER...

DOES ANYONE ELSE THINK IT'S *WEIRD* THAT IN ALL THESE *THOUSANDS OF MILES* OF DESERT...

...WE JUST *HAPPENED* TO FIND A GIANT WORM *AND* MR. FENSTER AT THE SAME PLACE AND THE SAME TIME?

THAT *IS* A PRETTY BIG COINCIDENCE!

HE SOUNDED LIKE HE'D FOUND SOMETHING *VALUABLE* THAT HE WANTED TO KEEP PEOPLE *AWAY* FROM. MAYBE, LIKE, A *NEW* FORTUNE IN AN *OLD* MINE?

SO HE HAS A REASON TO BE *HAPPY* ABOUT THE WORMS. JUST LIKE MR. WEST!

HEADS UP, GANG! I THINK WE'VE FOUND THE *START* OF OUR GIANT FRIEND'S SLIME TRAIL.

IT LOOKS LIKE THE ENTRANCE TO AN OLD ABANDONED *MINE!*

NEARLY *SEVEN FEET TALL*...BODY COVERED IN *MOSS* AND *SLIME*--!

LIKE *NOTHING* I'VE EVER SEEN BEFORE, BUT THE ONE THING I *DO* KNOW IS--

--IT DEFINITELY WASN'T *HUMAN!*

NO DISRESPECT, BUT I'M CERTAIN THIS *SWAMP MONSTER* OF YOURS WASN'T ACTUALLY *REAL.*

REAL OR NOT, A MONSTER LIKE *THAT* IS NOTHING TO *SNEEZE* AT!

THIS MANSION IS MY FAMILY *HOMESTEAD,* AND WAS LEFT TO *ME* IN MY MOTHER'S *WILL.* I'VE LIVED HERE MY *ENTIRE LIFE* AND CAN ASSURE YOU WE'VE NEVER HAD PROBLEMS WITH--!

KA-CHOO!

PERHAPS ONE OF YOUR *EMPLOYEES* IS BEHIND IT? WOULD IT BE POSSIBLE TO *SPEAK* WITH THEM?

I'M AFRAID MY *STAFF* HAVE ALL *QUIT.* IT SICKENS ME THAT THEY'D BE *SCARED OFF* BY A--!

HACK KA-CHOO KOFF

LOOKS LIKE YOU'RE NOT THE *ONLY* ONE WHO'S *SICKENED.*

HEY, VELMA--ARE YOU, LIKE, GONNA BE *OKAY?* WHAT'S *WRONG?*

IT'S *NOTHING.* JUST COMING DOWN WITH A *COLD...* OR THE *FLU.* I'LL BE FINE.

MR. HOLLANDER, MAY WE USE ONE OF YOUR *BEDROOMS?* MY FRIEND NEEDS TO *LIE DOWN.*

YES, OF COURSE. YOU'RE WELCOME TO USE *MY OWN* BEDROOM.

WHAT! THERE'S NO TIME FOR THIS! WE'VE GOT A MYSTERY TO SOLVE!

YOU'RE IN NO CONDITION TO DO ANYTHING BUT *REST.* WE CAN HANDLE THE *INVESTIGATION.*

BUT YOU NEED *ME* TO FIND *CLUES* AND LOCATE *WITNESSES!*

ARE YOU CERTAIN THAT *ALL* YOUR EMPLOYEES ARE GONE?

WELL...THERE IS A *FORMER* EMPLOYEE WHO MIGHT HAVE STAYED. MY OLD *GROUNDSKEEPER*--HE LIVES JUST OUTSIDE MY PROPERTY.

SEE THAT, VELMA? WE'VE GOT A POTENTIAL WITNESS ALREADY, SO JUST SIT BACK AND *RELAX!*

SURE! HOW AM I SUPPOSED TO *RELAX* WHEN YOU'RE HAVING ALL... ‡KA-CHOO!‡... THE *FUN?*

SHORTLY...

HEH! YOU KIDS DON'T *UNDERSTAND.* I'VE LIVED IN THIS NECK OF THE WOODS FOR NIGH ONTO *SIXTY YEARS*--I'VE SEEN *PLENTY* OF *STRANGE THINGS,* CAN YA BE MORE *SPECIFIC?*

WE CAN DO BETTER THAN THAT--WE'VE GOT *VISUALS!* SEE? HAVE YOU SEEN THIS *SWAMP MONSTER* LATELY?

SWAMP MONSTER! JUST LIKE THE YOUNG *HOLLANDER BOY* THOUGHT.

COME AGAIN?

MR. HOLLANDER UP IN THE MANSION HAS A *BROTHER* WHO HASN'T BEEN AROUND IN YEARS. WHEN THEY WERE LITTLE KIDDIES, THE *BROTHER* USED TO BELIEVE THERE WAS A *MONSTER* LIVING IN THE *SWAMP!*

KID HAD A WILD *IMAGINATION* AND WOULD MAKE UP *CRAZY STORIES*--!

WHAT KIND OF STORIES?

DID ANYONE ELSE HEAR THEM?

WAS HE PLAYING AROUND OR WAS HE SERIOUS?

DID HE EVER ACTUALLY SEE A MONSTER?

WHAT TH--? VELMA!!!

OKAY-- THAT'S ENOUGH EXCITEMENT FOR YOU! WE'RE TAKING YOU BACK TO THE MANSION.

BUT I DON'T WANT TO MISS ANYTHING!

THERE'S ONLY ONE THING TO SEE AROUND HERE--AND THERE HE IS NOW!

DARN! HE'S GETTING AWAY!

WE'LL CATCH UP WITH HIM LATER, FRED. RIGHT NOW WE'VE GOT TO TAKE CARE OF VELMA.

WE CAN'T GO CHASING AFTER A MONSTER AND LOOK AFTER YOU AT THE SAME TIME, VELMA. PROMISE ME YOU'LL STAY HERE, OKAY?

I PROMISE, DAPHNE. BUT I CAN'T PROMISE I CAN KEEP MY PROMISE!

SHAGGY, WE WANT YOU AND SCOOBY TO STAY HERE AND GUARD VELMA--MAKE SURE SHE STAYS IN BED!

HOPE YOU DON'T MIND-- IT'S THE ONLY WAY WE CAN GO MONSTER HUNTING WITHOUT HER FOLLOWING US!

WE GET TO LOAF AROUND WHILE YOU DO THE DANGEROUS WORK? ME AND SCOOB ARE, LIKE, THE PERFECT MEN FOR THE JOB!

OOH, THIS IS *RIDICULOUS!* I FEEL SO *USELESS!* WHAT AM I SUPPOSED TO DO WITH MYSELF WHILE I'M STUCK HERE?

GUESS I CAN DO A LITTLE *READING* TO HELP PASS THE TIME--!

BOY, THIS IS SOME COLLECTION OF BOOKS! I WONDER IF HOLLANDER KEEPS A *DIARY* OR A *FAMILY HISTORY*--?

KA-CHOO!!

GRRR! STUPID COLD IS MAKING ME CLUMSY!

WHAT'S THIS? *PAPERS* TUCKED AWAY INSIDE THE BOOK. *HOLLANDER'S* GOT SOMETHING TO *HIDE*...BUT WHAT?

A *WILL*... AND LEGAL DOCUMENTS ABOUT THE *MANSION.*

I DON'T SEE WHAT THE *BIG SECRET* IS, BUT MAYBE I'D BETTER TAKE A *CLOSER LOOK*--!

MAN, OH, MAN! I'M GLAD WE'RE NOT OUT MESSING WITH THAT SWAMP MONSTER, BUT I'M STARTING TO GET *BORED.*

RRRAND RRRUNGRY!

RRRUMBLE

YOU SAID IT, SCOOBY! AND HUNGRY! BUT WHAT TO DO ABOUT IT?

WOW! MR. HOLLANDER HAS THE MOST WELL-STOCKED KITCHEN I'VE EVER SEEN!

AT LEAST THAT'S ONE MYSTERY WE KNOW HOW TO SOLVE!

AND THE BEST PART IS WE'VE GOT IT ALL TO OURSELVES!

GLURRRGH...

GRRROARGH--!

BE PATIENT, SCOOB! IF YOU'RE GONNA MAKE A SANDWICH, YOU GOTTA DO IT PROPERLY! NOW PASS THE MUSTARD, WILL YA? THERE'S NOTHING SCARIER THAN A SANDWICH WITHOUT THE RIGHT--

RRRROARGH!!

--MUH-MUH-MONSTER? YOIKS!!!

THE END